A Very Unusual Dog

by
Dorothy Joan Harris

illustrations by
Kim LaFave

North Winds Press
A Division of Scholastic Canada Ltd.

The art style used in this book has evolved from the artist's oil and acrylic painting.
Characters and compositions are created in pencil. Then large sketches
are created and scanned into the computer, and colour is added digitally
using programs like Photoshop and Fractal Painter.

This book was typeset in 18 point Catull.

National Library of Canada Cataloguing in Publication

Harris, Dorothy Joan, 1931-
A very unusual dog / Dorothy Joan Harris ; illustrated by Kim LaFave.

ISBN 0-439-98977-9

I. LaFave, Kim II. Title.

PS8565.A6483V47 2004   jC813'.54   C2004-901357-2

6 5 4 3 2 1   Printed and bound in Canada   04 05 06 07 08

For Lisa and for John
– D.J.H.

For Michael and Tanya
– K.L.

"What are those toast crumbs doing on the windowsill?" asked Mother.

"I put them there," said Jonathan. "They're for my dog."

"We don't have a dog," said Elizabeth, who was seven and knew everything.

"I do," said Jonathan. "And he likes toast crumbs."

"That's silly," said Elizabeth. "Those toast crumbs will just sit there for days and then we'll get ants in the house and that will be yucky."

But the next morning the crumbs were gone.

At breakfast Jonathan said to Mother, "Please can we go to the park today? My dog wants to go."

"Dogs have to be on a leash in the park, you know," said Elizabeth.

"I know," said Jonathan.

When Jonathan put on his jacket he pulled out a long piece of rope with a little collar at the end of it.

"What's that for?" asked Mother.

"It's Dog's leash," said Jonathan.

"Dog?" said Elizabeth. "Hasn't he even got a proper name?"

"Yes. He's called Dog," said Jonathan.

"Well, if you're going to drag that silly thing along, I'm not walking with you," said Elizabeth.

So Elizabeth walked in front, with
Mother behind her, and Jonathan
and his dog behind them both.

Jonathan usually liked to go on the slide and the swings at the park. But today he just walked around.

"Don't you want to go on the slide?" asked Mother.

"No. Dog doesn't like slides. He just wants to walk around."

"We didn't need to come to the park to do that," Mother said.

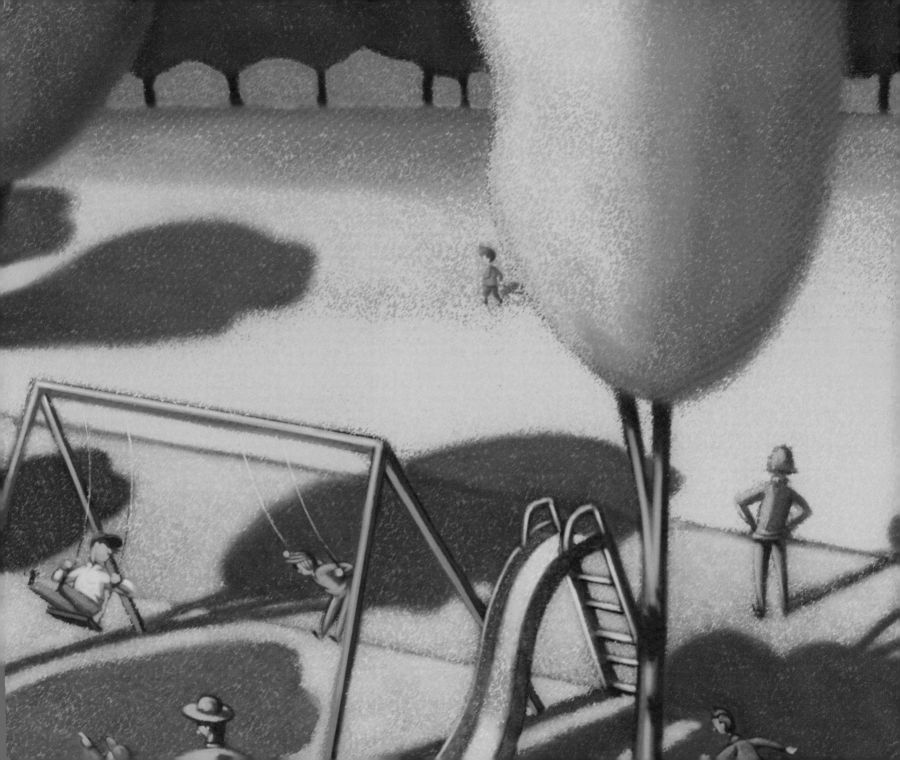

That evening when Elizabeth and
Jonathan were watching television,
Jonathan moved over to make
room for his dog.

"Dogs can't sit on the couch!"
said Elizabeth.

So Jonathan sat on the floor
instead, with his dog beside him.

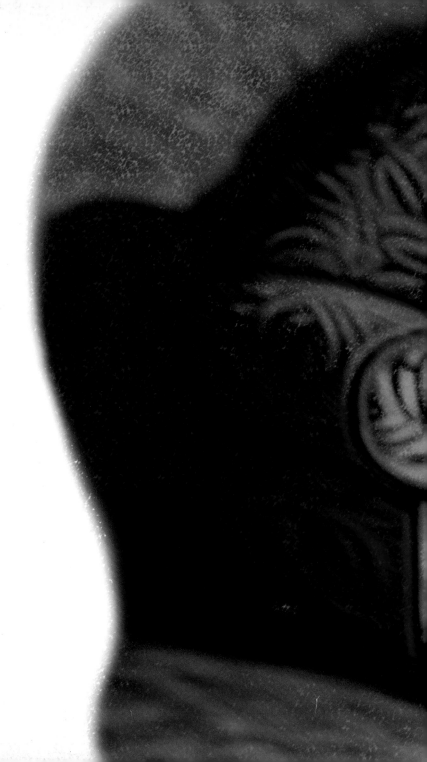

At bedtime Jonathan folded his sweater and put it on the floor beside his bed.

"What's your good sweater doing on the floor?" asked Mother.

"It's for Dog. He likes to sleep close to me," said Jonathan.

"He'll get dog hairs all over your sweater," said Elizabeth.

"I don't mind," said Jonathan.

15

For quite a few days Jonathan left crumbs on the windowsill, put his sweater beside his bed and took the rope to the park. On Sunday, when they were going to Grandma's apartment for dinner, Jonathan held the car door open for a long time.

"What are you doing?" asked Elizabeth.

"I'm letting Dog in the car," said Jonathan.

"He can't sit beside me," said Elizabeth. "He . . . he smells."

"He'll sit on the floor by my feet," said Jonathan.

At Grandma's Elizabeth said, "Jonathan's being silly.
He thinks he has a dog. It has to go everywhere with him."

"Oh," said Grandma. "What kind of dog?"

"He's got long ears and a soft coat," said Jonathan.
"His name's Dog."

"He's not a *real* dog, you know," said Elizabeth.

"Well . . . he sounds like a spaniel," said Grandma. She
looked in her desk drawer and took out a photograph. It
showed a dog with long ears sitting with a big fluffy cat.
"Does he look like this?" she asked.

Jonathan studied the photo. "Yes, that's what he looks like," he said. "Was this your dog?"

"No, that was the dog that lived next door to me. The cat was mine," said Grandma. "She used to play with the dog. She was a very unusual cat."

"What happened to her?" asked Jonathan.

"She got old and died," said Grandma.

"Why don't you get another cat?" asked Jonathan.

"I can't. The apartment building doesn't allow pets," said Grandma.

"Do you miss her?"

"Sometimes."

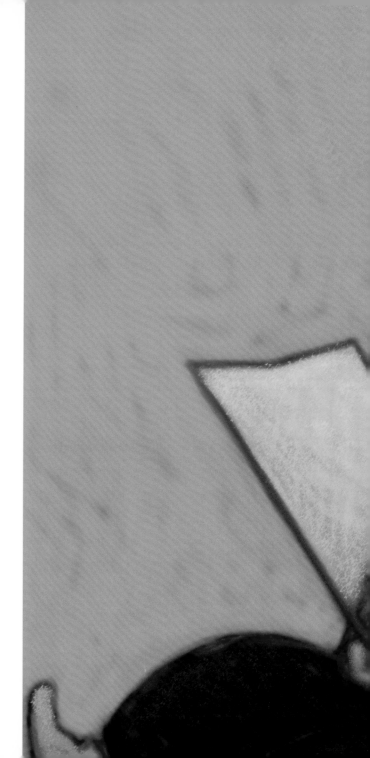

It was late when they left Grandma's. Jonathan fell asleep in the car, and his father carried him up to bed.

The next morning Jonathan ate all his toast without leaving any crumbs. Elizabeth watched him.

"Aren't you going to feed that dog of yours?" she asked.

"No," said Jonathan. "I left him at Grandma's. I think she was lonely for a pet."

"I don't believe you," said Elizabeth, and she went to the phone.

"Did Jonathan leave Dog at your apartment?" she asked Grandma.

"Dog?" said Grandma.

"Yes. Jonathan said he left his dog with you because you were lonely," explained Elizabeth.

"Well . . . yes, he did," said Grandma. "And Dog slept by my bed all night. Ask Jonathan what he likes to eat."

Jonathan went to the phone.

"He likes toast crumbs best," he told Grandma.

"I'll remember that," said Grandma.

"And he likes to go for walks. I had a leash for him."

"I'll remember that too," said Grandma.

"And you know what, Grandma?"
said Jonathan. "If you want, you can even
call him Cat. He won't mind. He's a very
unusual dog."